Anatoli Scholz

Seven Nights in Berlin

Second edition

Cover & illustrations by Marion Garnier
Edited by James Magniac

www.anatolischolz.com

For Tom & Tima & all the other dancers

Then one day it all came to an end... It was that simple, it ended so abruptly that I failed to grasp the enormity of what had happened...

Sabahattin Ali

Nights

Tuesday*

*in Berlin, the weeks start on a Tuesday

Tuesday

Standing in front of the bathroom mirror of the *Galerie König* I could barely recognize myself. A week in Berlin had given me more than I could have ever understood on a first sober Tuesday morning. Tears tickled their way onto my face and mixed with the little mascara I had on. I looked different. Not in any bad way, but different.

My mind was still clouded by the flashes and beats from the weekend. I tried to stop crying, as I had no reason to but felt overwhelmed. The bathroom's unaggressive white walls were piercing my head. I kept staring at my reflection as if I would fall into it, until I had a fleeting thought about writing my ex. That's when I knew it had to do with the ecstasy.

I remembered Josie's nonchalant warning about the delayed emotional comedown while we were preparing to go out on Saturday. She rattled off some side effects while holding a *Berliner Pils* bottle in one hand and a pill of ecstasy in the other. As soon as she was done with her warning, she bit into the pill and handed me the rest.

I didn't hesitate to take what was offered, nor did anyone else. Down went the rabbit into its hole, and we all followed, promptly. No one stopped to point out that the vermin didn't have to live until next week. But we did.

I washed my face in the sink and returned to my desk behind the ticket counter of the gallery. I had not been bestowed with any real tasks yet, punching tickets, swiping cards, and handing out brochures. My weeping escape went by unnoticed.

Josie worked in the bookshop across the narrow lobby from where I was seated. She had lived in Berlin for a few years and had declared herself a sort of guide for me. It was comforting to have her know what was wrong with me this Tuesday. She walked over to the front desk after lunch. My head was still throbbing.

"Luce, cancel all your plans for tonight!" she yelled at me

across the counter, a bright lip-glossed smile sparkling between her golden loop earrings. No sign of suffering on her. "Greg is throwing a house party; you're coming!"

"Cancel my plans ...?" I replied. "How are you ... thinking about doing anything already?" I could hear my speech drag.

Josie held out her index finger and then reached into her wallet. "Wait ... here, I've got something for you! It's called 5-HTP and it restores endorphins or something like that. Take it and you'll feel much better," handing me a white capsule.

It looked less menacing than the pills from the weekend. I stared for a second as it lay on the dark glass counter in front of me.

"Wait Josie, did you say Greg? As in Greg *Franken*?" I finally registered what she had said.

"The one and only!" Josie smiled at me. "I know you've been wanting to meet him. This is your chance!"

"Oh no! I mean ... yes, of course ... but why does it have to be today?" I looked up at Josie, recognizing the same devilish seduction from Saturday.

"I'm sending you the address. You're coming! Take the pill, eat something, have a nap, and you'll be fine!" She winked at me and turned on her heel to return to the bookshop before I even had the time to reply.

Josie knew that Greg Franken was one of the reasons why I chose to work for *König's*. I needed to stop suffering, I needed to get to that party, and I needed to stop thinking about my ex. It seemed Berlin wasn't giving me a break just yet.

I gulped down Josie's new pill with a glass of water and followed it with a halloumi sandwich I bought from the Lebanese shop across the street.

When I got home from work, I crashed on my bed and fell asleep the moment my head touched the pillow, waking up half an hour later feeling excited. Whether it was the 5-HTP, the anticipation, or the power nap, Suicide Tuesday would not have me any longer. It was time to pick an outfit for the party.

My closet was still a mess since I had moved in. Most of my clothes lay in a pile atop my trusty suitcase, the combined result of last weekend's dress-picking frenzy and my stubborn devotion to chaos. I liked to think that it was the burden of an artist to be this messy. I also liked to think that it forced me to find patterns in everyday things, an obsessive weapon against boredom.

That night, my chaos worked against me, and I started to feel anxious about the party and Greg Franken. I scrambled to find my black Kookaï dress, adding the black Docs and throwing on my overcoat before rushing outside. The classics. A quick check in the hallway mirror assured me that I was starting to look more like the old Lucy again. Josie had sent me another message, asking me whether I was already on my way.

The location was a short walk up *Warschauer Straße*, which gave me the opportunity to realize how much of my new neighborhood I had gotten to know. After all, a week ago, I had walked up *Warschauer* and not known left from right. A few daily walks later, and I had started to recognize the shapes of the cobblestone under my feet, the snowed-in flowerpots lining the wall of the Sparkasse, and the silly cat curtains in the windows of the pet shop. It was far from home, but my Berlin canvas was getting its first layer. I was starting to see some direction here.

I rubbed my hands as I looked for the doorbell outside house number 54. I rang "Franken" and was immediately buzzed in, without anyone coming on the intercom.

Impatient to meet one of my idols, I rushed to the top floor. I could hear music coming through the half-opened door as I passed the final flight of stairs, my heart pounding from exhaustion, and pushed it open.

Facing the door as I stepped into the apartment, a peculiar

9

couple was awaiting my entrance. I had just enough time to turn my panting face into a smile as both men jumped at me, swinging their arms around my shoulders.

"Welcome! You are a winner!" one of the men exclaimed, giving me a kiss on the cheek. "We love you!"

"We love you!" Joined the other.

"Love you … too …?" I muttered short of breath. A second kiss landed on my other cheek. "Should I take off my …" I just had time to ask, stopping midsentence, as I was already being led inside.

As I was escorted between the two men, I made a note of their outfits. The couple was stripped down to their black leather underwear, which was suspended by alternating neon green or yellow straps, and they walked on pink platform shoes. One was blonde and the other brunette, with either face covered in rainbow-colored glitter. I knew this was Berlin, but still had a hard time not asking about their getup, until we walked out of the corridor.

We arrived in front of a massive room, standing on a deck by the entryway that led down to where the action was happening. On the left side, lowered into the ground, a small DJ deck was playing the ambient tracks that the room was submerged in. The furniture, pots, and decorations all bore black or dark-red colors. It gave the apartment a distinctly pornographic feel. I was instantly entranced by the mix of swaying colors and music. This was exactly how I imagined Greg to live.

My brunette friend tugged at my coat. I handed it to him, thinking about where my Kookaï placed me in the room as I was left standing alone on the deck.

There were at least two dozen people dotting the massive room. A few of them were also dressed in kinky clothes, like my welcoming duo. Some wore classic attire, with button-down shirts and dark cocktail dresses. At first look, I could not make

10

out Josie or what I thought might have been Greg.

That's when I noticed the few brightly colored objects placed in between the people and the furniture. I knew they had to be Greg's works. Statues of human silhouettes bent in all kinds of inhumane positions he used for his augmented reality exhibitions.

I heard Josie call my name and turned to see her run up to me. She was wearing a sports bra top and washed-out jeans.

"You made it! Feeling better?" Her eyes were twinkling with excitement. She gave me a hug.

"I do! I took a nap; that really helped," I answered.

"Naps, naps, naps … I tell you, they save lives!" Josie smiled from ear to ear. "Have some of this, and let me find Greg for you!" She handed me a glass of white wine and took my arm to lead me down to the room.

"Are you sure he won't mind?" I asked, growing increasingly unsure about all the forced guidance.

"Oh shush! What do you think of his place?" She let go of my arm and twirled in front of me in the middle of the room. "Isn't it majestic?"

I took a look around and noted the statues again, this time from close up.

"Yes … it's huge! These are all his, right?" I asked, pointing to the figure that had already caught my eye from the beginning. It looked like a young cupid, whose bow and arrow had been replaced with binoculars strapped around his neck.

"Ah, yes. *Blooming Youth*," spoke a deep voice from my left.

I turned around and saw a big-bellied, middle-aged man standing in front of me. Wearing an almost completely undone silk shirt and wide 1950s-style pants, his most remarkable feature had to be his perfectly round face. Adding to his black-rimmed round glasses and overall round figure, he made an utterly comical appearance. This was our host.

"There you are, Greg!" said Josie. "I was just looking for you! You have to meet my newest colleague from the gallery, Lucy. She just moved to Berlin."

Still in slight shock since my arrival and Greg's sudden appearance, I held my breath.

"Hi there, Lucy," he reached out his hand. "I'm Greg Franken. Hope you are enjoying my little get-together." He put on an absent smile while his eyes wandered around the room behind me.

I instinctively reached out for Greg's hand and felt his grasp release me from my stupor.

"It's such a pleasure to meet you! Thank you so much for the invite! I am a big admirer of your work," I blurted all out at once, which seemed to focus his eyes back to me. He smiled again, this time more sincerely.

"You seem to have a good eye." Greg pointed to the statue of the cupid. "Not a lot of people notice this one at first, but it's one of my favorites."

Greg's step toward the cupid seemed to invite me to come closer to the pedestal of the two-foot-tall statue. He held still in front of it and didn't seem to notice as I approached next to him. Josie turned away from us and jumped in with the people dancing in front of the DJ.

"You said, *'Blooming Youth'*?" I asked quietly. "What does it mean?"

"Are you familiar with one Leopold Bloom from Joyce's *Ulysses*?" Greg replied without moving his gaze from the cupid. His voice was soothing, dragging out the long U sounds of the words.

"I'm afraid I've never read it." I felt embarrassed.

"Ah, you see, it's a marvelous story!" He reached out to touch the head of the statue. "It plays out in one ordinary day of a particular Mr. Bloom in Dublin. As often the case with turn-of-

12

the-century novelists, the book is about everything and nothing at the same time. Mr. Bloom faces a dozen obstacles, and yet, nothing is revealed to us. We are left with the same questions as when we started. So, why even read it?"

As he stopped talking, he finally turned to me, pushing his sliding glasses back up to the arch of his nose with his middle finger. I was so surprised by his attention that I was not sure if he expected me to say something.

"Aha," I said, trying to see past the reflections of his spectacles, "but what does it have to do with the cupid?"

"Let me ask you this, Lucy. Does it make you think of anything?" Greg asked, turning back to his subject.

I took a look around the room, consciously stopping myself from rubbing my temples. The warmth of the room reminded me of my trying day, and a slight headache set in again. Just like the previous days, this had all been a little overwhelming. That's when it came to me.

"Aimlessness," I replied. "Aimless quests for love, perhaps?"

"Yes," Greg spoke softly, now stroking the head of the cupid. "We are all aimless. It may be at love, our youth, or this party."

He turned to me once more and gave me one big smile. He then reached out his other hand and put it on my head, starting to stroke it, too, rolling his eyes into the back of his head, as if to transfer energy between the cupid and me.

It must have been a common sight for Greg's guests, as no one reacted to the spectacle. I calmed my nerves by taking a sip from the wine that Josie had given me, with no other idea on how to handle this moment.

Greg let go of both of us after a few seconds. He seemed more elated than before and even let go a chuckle that made his entire body jiggle.

I had to think back on my weekend. Was Greg high? In that millisecond between deciding whether I should ask him more questions or not, I wondered if this was what all of Berlin was like. I gathered up my courage.

"I've admired your work for so long," I said. "I would love to hear more from you about your process. Maybe not now ... if you don't have the time."

Greg looked at me, still wearing a grin from his self-inflicted chuckle.

"You know, the thing about my statues is that I don't think anyone sees them anymore. They scroll through them like they scroll through articles on their smartphone. Look around! No one is here to see them. They are just paying attention to themselves." He waved his hands around the room and ended with pointing both of his index fingers at me.

"What do you mean?" I was surprised by this remark. "Aren't you famous for them?"

"That is precisely my worry." Greg closed his eyes and tilted his head up. "We live off of our glory days. We become famous for being famous. That's when we lose track of our art. No one can truly exist without engaging with the present world. What are those old glories worth today? They are as gone as their creators. A new creator needs new worlds."

Greg stood half turned toward me and half turned toward the crowd where Josie was dancing with her arms up. I wondered whether he really meant what he said. He opened his eyes again and looked back at me. We made eye contact, and I could sense he felt my bewilderment. I looked back at the cupid.

"Why binoculars?" I asked.

"That's the right question!" He gestured at Josie. "Let's ask Josie ... my darling!" She looked up and skipped toward us right away.

"What's up, my lovelies? You aren't arguing already, I hope?" She smirked, looking more and more exuberant. Pearls of sweat had built up on her forehead from the dancing.

"Your friend here asked why the cupid has binoculars. What do you think?" Greg asked her.

"Who needs a bow and arrow anyway?" Josie countered his question, giggling.

"Aha! But there's more to it! Hold on ..." Greg gestured for Josie to hold still. He reached into his deep pocket and pulled out two sets of goggles and a remote. He handed the glasses to Josie and me. "Put them on."

We followed his instruction. The goggles were practically see-through and were concave around the edges. I put them on and watched Greg press a button on the remote. Everything turned black.

I let out a gasp, reaching for the goggles, thinking something had gone wrong. But then, in the blink of an eye, white outlines of figures began to draw themselves through the darkness. I kept looking. It did not take me long to understand that the outlines were the forms of Greg's statues and the only thing visible through these goggles. However, instead of being static, the statues were moving and seemed alive in this reality. I saw the figures bending, galloping, and swimming across the giant room. The rest of the party, the people and the furniture, had all but disappeared. This was Greg's world.

"Look for the cupid," I heard Greg say.

Sure enough, there he was, right in front of me. The little cupid, sitting on his rock with his folded wings, holding the binoculars in his hands. His face looked more desperate in this world. At times, he would get up on his rock and look through the binoculars. He turned all around like the sailor on the mast of his galleon, then lowering his binoculars and his head. The cycle repeated itself every few seconds. He got up, looked around, sat back down, and sank his head. A few moments later, and he would get up to look again.

I kept watching until everything turned off. I took off the

goggles and handed them back to Greg. The party came back into focus. The cupid was back in his place, immobile.

"Did you see him?" asked Greg, putting the goggles back into his pocket.

"Yes," Josie and I answered simultaneously.

"What did you see?" he asked.

"He was looking for something," said Josie.

"What do you think it was?" he asked.

"Something new," I said.

"Precisely," said Greg.

Wednesday

Adriana handed me the deck of tarot cards. I shuffled through them, running my fingers over their golden edges. The evening sun drew long shadows of each object on the table between us.

"Think of who you are at this exact moment," she said. "Close your eyes … focus … put your energy into the cards. And give them back to me."

I did as I was told.

Adriana had come from far away to visit me for a few days. As I announced her visit to my flatmate Fred, I introduced her as the only person I had ever known with her unique devotion to nature, often talking about the capricious characters of plants, follies of trees, and their energy.

In short, I had been looking forward to hosting her in Berlin and see her floral spirit dropped into the deep end of my urban existence. It had been a tough few weeks between the trips to see my family up north and staying focused on finishing the design for the Daimler interface. Her arrival balanced perfectly against the dread of midweek assignments. It was on her second day that she took out the tarot cards.

The day prior, I had finished work early so we could go see the exhibit on German Romanticism in the *Alte Nationalgalerie*. In her presence, I was immediately reminded of what I had been missing. Adriana spent twenty minutes staring at the infamous *Wanderer over the Sea of Fog* by Friedrich in the main hall. She didn't simply stand in front of it slack-jawed but rather moved and swung around the painting, inspecting it from all possible angles. While she did that, I sat down and watched her scan it, pan away, and then look up at it again, as if engaged in conversation. She was talking with the faceless Wanderer without saying a word.

I agreed to her reading my cards because of what I had seen in the gallery. I wasn't sure what I had witnessed, but it had

21

been the last time I had seen someone stare at something for twenty minutes that wasn't a smartphone. One thing was for sure: she seemed to know something I didn't.

Adriana took back the deck and laid out ten cards on the table in front of me. The rings on her hands clinked together as she sorted the cards. She had always worn a lot of jewelry, but this time, it seemed more appropriate than ever.

A silver headband with mustard-colored pendants in the shape of olive tree leaves lay over her dark-brown hair. It felt as if Princess Scheherazade herself had come to read for me accompanied by a melody. Four or five silver coins hung from the triangular metallic forms that were her earrings. Each time she moved her head, they rang together softly.

She began the reading seemingly unaware of my fascination. To do so, she would turn over a card, look at me, pause for a moment, and then speak. I had the impression that she was hesitant. I recognized the same care she had given the *Wanderer* in the gallery. Her words were carefully chosen, but once she spoke, there was no doubt in her voice.

The cards yielded some expected results:

"You need to control your emotions," read the Seven of Cups.

"There was a great challenge in your past you still need to deal with," was the message of the Hermit.

"Stay loyal to your friends but know who is true to you," said the Ten of Swords.

When we got to the fourth one, Adriana turned it over and did not look up. I kept my eyes on her and saw her expression change to an uncharacteristic frown, her pendants losing their reflection. I looked down and read the name of the card: "Death."

"This isn't a very nice card," she said.

"You don't say?" I smiled, trying to make light of the situation.

"It's not bad …" Adriana looked up and tried to return my

smile. "It doesn't mean that you'll die or anything. It just means you have dealt or will deal with death somehow. It's very vague like that. Don't take it as a bad omen!"

"Should I worry?" I asked.

"Well, no! Of course not! You know that these cards don't read the future," she said, turning her palms up and leaning her head forward, allowing a soft ring from the coins. "You interpret into them whatever is going through your head. Is there anything that you're thinking about now?"

I wondered for a second as Adriana widened her eyes. I had nothing to hide.

"I guess ... my grandmother." I said the first thing that came to mind. "She died a month ago ..."

Adriana looked at me with no pity, as if she had expected the response. She took a deep breath and gestured for me to put my hands in hers, closed her eyes, and clenched my fingers tightly. A few seconds later, she looked up again and smiled. I smiled back.

"Wine?" I asked in a renewed attempt to lighten the mood. "Are we allowed to drink while doing this?"

Adriana nodded.

I brought in a bottle my father had gifted me on my last visit, and the card reading continued without any further grim interruptions. I became entertained by the reading, knowing that I wasn't finding any truths, yet there was something unexpected happening, something else. I was allowing myself to be part of my own story again. Every time Adriana spoke, I felt an invitation to relive a distinct memory, not unlike a lucid dream, unfolded, with me as the unaffected spectator.

As we progressed into the evening, I kept watching Adriana's jewelry and behavior. She continued to take thoughtful pauses after turning each card. When she started each explanation, she would move her head forward, gazing deeply into my eyes.

In that moment, her earrings would fall forward and ring like a timed wind chime. The entire nature of the setup gave me a sense of importance. I could see that she was giving a lot of herself to me and wondered how often she had done this, as it seemed quite a feat for both of us. I also wondered how long this importance would last.

As if the cards had heard me, the door to the room burst open. In came my flatmate Fred, carrying so much energy with him that I had to assume that he was drunk. I turned and was still shaking off the build-up before realizing he was already by our table.

"Looks like you guys are having fun without me!" he bellowed, throwing his coat on the couch and walking over to open a window.

His loud noises and clumsy steps clashed with the calmer aura Adriana and I had been set in. I didn't mind and was even relieved, as we were ripe for a shake-up. Fred kissed Adriana and me hello.

"Adriana has just been warning me about some things in my future," I said.

Fred raised his eyebrows. "You? Didn't think you'd be into this sort of stuff! Never thought I'd catch you dead with a fortune-teller. How the hell did you get him to do this?" He laughed.

Adriana and I looked at each other. She shrugged her shoulders with a coy smile.

"It's been good fun," I shrugged along. "A glass, Freddie?"

"I would love to but really shouldn't," he replied.

"Ah! Really?" Adriana had a smirk on her face.

"Hey now! Hey! I have to get up early tomorrow morning, all right? Don't go on about me. You're the ones in this weird, sexual fortune-reading session." Fred got up with attitude and raised his voice. "I remember doing things like that, babe, OK? Going out on a weekday and getting wasted! Been there and

24

done that, honey!"

Fred's antics made us burst out in laughter as he struck a pose in front of us. Adriana had to put her glass down, and I got light-headed from trying to contain myself, both of us roaring.

"Well, I'm going to go make myself some tea, at least. Another bottle?" Fred pointed to the nearly emptied wine to receive an enthusiastically musical nod from Adriana. He was almost through the door when I stopped him.

"Wait," I caught my breath. "Do you have some ketamine left over from the weekend?"

Fred looked a little surprised but grinned back with a quick, "Yeah, sure," before disappearing through the door. Adriana didn't comment on it, pouring herself another glass and thus finishing the bottle.

I got up to put on some music to match the new mood of the room, putting on Sama's *Boiler Room* set. Just like Adriana's jewelry, the cards, and the ketamine, I was looking to fit the details of an inexplicable evening into a formed image.

Fred came back a few moments later, handing me a small folded paper pocket and pouring me a new glass of wine. While I handled the K, I looked over at Adriana a few times. She did not seem concerned, even though she spared a few curious glances.

"Do you want some?" I asked both of them. They shook their heads and continued their conversation that Fred has started about the fine wine he had brought in. Sama' was just getting started when I took my line through a rolled up twenty-euro note.

It hit me later than usual. I was watching the reddening sky through the opened window, listening to the kettle boiling in the background as my breath widened. Those two kept talking and laughing while my world started to slow down and I elongated. In an instant, my mind had escaped my body and had taken refuge in one of the upper corners of the room. Adriana and

Fred had disappeared into the distance, and I saw myself and the scenario in which I had left my body.

I saw myself sitting at a table with ten cards laid out in front of my seated figure. Just minutes ago, those cards were revealed to me for the first time and had already acclaimed immense importance. I felt their gravity and tried to concentrate on that feeling. Adriana came into focus again. It had been her energy after all; her energy commanded the cards.

I stretched out my left hand and played an invisible piano with my fingers. In that motion, I ran it across one of the cards on the table and picked it up without thinking. Hearing some chatter in the background, I understood that Adriana and Fred were probably talking about me. What they didn't know was that they were watching me the same way I was watching myself. I wasn't in my own body … at least not fully.

I looked at the card the hand had picked up. It had a beautiful drawing of a dark silhouette sitting in a wooden boat with its back turned to the viewer. It reminded me of the *Wanderer* who had made such an impact on Adriana. It was a shame it had to be called Death. I tried to remember what Adriana had said about it but couldn't. All I could think of was how she had stared at the *Wanderer* in the gallery. How she had communicated with the faceless. She must have known about the resemblance in her tarot deck, maybe even felt my misfortune. I placed the card back on the table.

"How's it feelin'?" I heard Fred ask.

My head turned to him. I felt amused by his question but tried to answer earnestly. The big high was starting to wear off. I leaned back into my chair but kept levitating.

"Good." I smiled. "Really fun."

"Explain it to me, Chris," Adriana asked. "I've never done it."

"You haven't? Oh …" I replied, with my eyes closed. "Let me tell you what it feels like … It feels like something soft … I am

26

encapsulated in a sort of cocoon. I swim in it … When I am about to hit a wall, I bounce. Gravity teases me down and I … I resist. That's the best I can explain."

I opened my eyes and was at once attracted by a purple gemstone on one of Adriana's rings. That left hand was curled around her wine glass, making the dimming light from the window sparkle across all of its shiny surfaces. I averted my eyes and, falling back to the card, knew what would happen before it did. The hooded silhouette drew me back.

"What is it, Chris? You keep looking at that card," said Fred. "What does it say?"

He got up from his chair and leaned over.

"Death? Fuck, guys! What have you been dealing with here? I thought this was about … you know … winning money or finding a soulmate. No wonder you needed some ket!" He sounded sarcastic but turned to Adriana expecting a response.

"It's not that bad. It's just a card for you to deal with death," said Adriana.

"Oh, so this is interesting." Fred turned to me. "Chris. What do you think about death while high on ketamine?"

I looked at Fred and then Adriana. I knew that Fred had to be kidding, asking me that question then.

"You start," I answered. "You start, and then I'll go."

"I don't mind," said Adriana. She looked upbeat, taking another sip of wine and pulling up in her seat. "I actually have a theory. To me, death is not scary. I think about it quite a lot. A lot more than when I was younger, and it does not scare me so much anymore. I see it just like I see this card. It's just one of many in the deck. It's one of the most devastating ones, but it has to be in there. Otherwise, the deck would be incomplete. Life would be incomplete."

"You're crazy, girl." Fred interjected. "You think about death? Like, the disappearance of everything? Like, how everything goes away? That doesn't scare you?"

"Yes! Why should it?" she smiled proudly.

"You're crazy. No, not for me," said Fred. "I ignore it as much as I can! If I don't, I would end up depressed. I know I have this beautiful life and only one at that. I want to be able to look forward to those things that I know I can have: my wine, good food, sex. Not being scared of death? You'd have to be drunk, in love, or a moron. Are you any of those, Adriana? Or all three?"

We all laughed with Fred once more. My high had passed, and I was mostly back in my own body. While Fred was speaking, I was preparing what I wanted to give as my answer and became thankful that Fred had teased me. My thoughts felt quite original, and I doubted whether I would have had them sober.

"I think the card shows death the right way," I finally said while the others were still giggling. "We don't see death's face. Whether he is on a boat, on a hilltop, or at your bedside. We won't know his face until he is here. And then it's too late, anyway."

"So, what does that mean?" asked Adriana. "If we don't see his face, we should be scared of him?"

"I don't know," I replied. "I guess there is just this path ahead of him. That's the only place where you can see his face."

"I like that," said Adriana.

"Yes, very pretty, Chris," added Fred. "It took you a line of ket to become a poet. So maybe there is no need to be afraid. But that's not a reason to talk about it too much. Agreed?"

Fred looked over at Adriana. She had started to pack up the deck in front of me, giving him a seductive look.

"Do you want me to read your cards now, Fred?" she asked.

Thursday

Thursday

I *don't think I will ever know why you can't be happy. And neither will you.* Beth's words rang in my head as I hung on to the bar. The pint of beer glued to the copper counter, my hand glued to the glass.

Everything in front of me had become blurry from the fourth or fifth drink I was having. My workday and walk to Südkreuz had already slipped into a forgotten past, and I had to take another look around to remind myself of where I was, if only to distract myself from that goddamn statement.

The copper counter under my glass extended into the typical black walls and mirrored background with the booze on display. Behind the bar, the barman threw his head back at something that a girl in a skimpy blue dress had said to him. Behind me, seated at the table below my stool, a girl's loud small talk about art galleries seemed to force her into sprawling her elbows over the tabletop. The window table had a group of five with matching backpacks at their feet, all sheathed in their phones. None of it held my interest for too long.

"Are you alright, *gordito*? Sammy?" I heard Chippy ask.

"He doesn't look good," added Clarisse.

I had somehow overlooked my own two friends sitting right next to me. I looked up at them with one eye open under a raised eyebrow.

"Of course." I smiled. "Everything's fine."

"*Hermano*, you look like shit. I don't believe you," said Chippy, putting his heavy arm on my shoulder. I turned back to the bar. The bartender nodded at me instinctively, but I lifted my still half-full beer in gratitude.

Chippy and Clarisse were being nice by getting me to come out, and I hated turning my back to them. There is nothing more depressing than seeing yourself be ungrateful to someone who is simply being kind. I just couldn't handle their dynamic. Chippy, with his energetic demeanor would turn the world for me to feel better before he would understand that it's impossible. His girlfriend, Clarisse, I wasn't even sure enjoyed being here with him, much less with me. I had to pull myself together not to start throwing attitude at their questions and saying things I would regret.

It came back to me that Mike had also been with us, and I wondered where he had disappeared to. He was the one actually drinking with me. Chippy was the one who told us to come out but hadn't had a sip.

"Where did Mike go?" I asked.

"He said he'll be right back. Chill!" Chippy yelled at me, getting up.

"Where the fuck is Mike?" I yelled back.

Sinking back down, I covered my head with my hands. It had started spinning in a rush, and I felt another pat on my shoulder. I just wanted Mike to get back to drinking with me, to drowning sorrows, and to pointless male banter.

It was all Beth's fault, anyway. She had shattered any remaining pride two days prior when she asked me if she could fuck the actor she met at *Alte Münze*. I still saw her innocent face in front of me as she asked me if I would be okay with it. Some bullshit argument about polyamory. I called her greedy, even though I could have said worse things.

My thoughts were suddenly interrupted by a lot of noise coming from the entrance of the bar. I lifted my head, squinting at the door just in time to see a group of matching buttoned-up gentlemen step in. A stag night, without a doubt. I looked to the barman, who made no effort to hide his eye roll.

"It's all right, you can stop petting me," I said to Chippy. "Just turn in, and I'll wait for Mike."

"*Hermano*, maybe we should all go home together," Chippy replied. "Let's watch a movie or something."

"Oh, oh, oh! Guys!" One of the buttoned-up gentlemen

crossed half the bar when he heard Chippy speak. "You're French, aren't you? No, no, no … let me guess! Don't say it … Italian!" He was pointing his finger at my friend. Another member of the stags had followed him to both end up standing right next to us. A moment of silence turned into a clear hesitation from Chippy to respond. The tension mounted so quickly that I had momentarily regained full control of my vision and motor senses.

"Sorry?" Chippy replied.

"Italian, right? Where are you from?" The grinner insisted.

"I am from Berlin." Chippy replied sternly.

Clarisse took a step next to him, and he added, "She's from Berlin too. And him!" he said, pointing at me.

The other guy shouldered his questioning predecessor, looping his arm around him. "No, no, guys. He means, where are you *really* from?"

I could see Chippy's eyes turning fiery, a cog of warring responses slowing itself by force. Maybe it was because he had been taking care of me. His heart was in the right place that night. Chippy smiled, looked down at the floor, and answered without making eye contact. "I was born in Zaragoza, Spain."

"Ah, that's what I meant! 'Cause I can hear a little accent! You're all Spanish?" The question seemed to be directed at Clarisse.

"Paris," she answered, taking a sip of my beer, looking aside.

The two responded with a baffled look at each other before the first one returned with a machine-gun round of questioning.

"Paris? You're French? But you speak English with each other? How does that even work? How is that possible? My girlfriend and I can't understand each other, and we are from the same village. I mean, what do you speak when you get in a fight?"

I listened quietly, letting an all too familiar row of disbelief wash over us. I had to admit to being relieved by the shift of

35

focus away from me but could have been spared the drunk stag posse.

"I scream in French," said Clarisse, making me for once admire that dismissive sass in her voice. "*Oh, c'est* Mike!" Her second statement added relief to my admiration.

Chippy stood up around the two men, pushing them to a muffled protest of "Oh, oh, careful," until they understood that they were no longer part of our conversation. They waved their hands at Chippy, readjusting their shirts, but departed as unceremoniously as they had appeared.

Meanwhile, I watched Mike shuffle his silly grin between the tables to get to the bar, oblivious to any tension hanging in the air. He walked straight toward me, ordered us both another beer, and only then turned to Chippy and Clarisse.

"Did I miss anything?" he asked with the broadest of smiles.

"You have got to be kidding me," Chippy laughed, turning to Clarisse. "OK, I think we should go."

Clarisse answered by giving him a deserving kiss.

"Oh, really? What *did* I miss?" Mike looked at me, but I decided to give an innocent shrug as our friends hugged us goodbye.

"Don't worry about it," I added once they were gone.

He sat down in Chippy's seat, patiently waiting for our drinks to arrive while looking at something on his phone. There was something in Mike's company that made me feel as if I was the one doing him a favor by being there. Call it the unconditional love of your drunk uncle. He will calmly accompany you without judgement or any real interest altogether. It was the nicest sentiment I could have been feeling. Most of the stag party had moved outside for a smoke, the barman was back at drying the glasses, and the couple next to us had finally moved on to touching each other's hands. I wasn't about to credit it all to Mike's presence, but somehow, it was when he was around that things lost their needless complication.

Maybe Beth had been right, maybe I just didn't have this natural calmness, an ability to switch into second gear and just be happy with myself. I never thought of it as something desirable, surviving in this new world where everything is protected under a noble mindfulness. I couldn't look past that simple obsessive question: one actor and then what? After the actor, the doctor, the lawyer, the rabbi? I could only wish to control these thoughts before they took their own velocity inside my brain, wished for a cut and the next scene.

As if he had felt it, Mike burst into my observation of the couple with a fresh glass of beer. I smiled and nodded, raising the drink to my lips and seeking his eye contact.

"Do you think I was wrong?" I asked Mike after a gulp. "I mean, I could've learned to live with Beth like this ... right? Who knows?"

He shook his head. "Man, shut up! Here, look at this. " Mike swiped for something on his phone and turned it toward me. "This will get your mind off of it."

There was a girl on his screen, standing in front of a mirror, taking a picture of herself, her hips turning into a naked waist and torso. Her breasts exposed and only her face and backdrop indistinguishable.

"Wow!" I exclaimed, reaching to grab the phone, but Mike jerked it back. "Wait, wait! Let me take another look! She's super hot. Who is she? Does she have friends?"

"Get in line, man," he said, winking.

"But ... wait, this isn't the same one you showed me last week?" I asked.

He shook his head.

"How many does this make?"

"Dunno, like, four," he answered.

"For fuck's sake, that's a lot! How do they not know of each other?" I lay my head in my palm. "How do you manage?"

"Honestly, I have no idea. The less I think about it, the better."

I looked at him.

"Are you happy, Mike?" I smirked.

He smiled but did not answer. He looked at his glass, took it, and turned to me to cheer. I thought I heard him mutter, "Happy, happy," under his breath before he drank. I should have been asked that question but couldn't blame Mike. He was a good man, something he could do nothing about.

"I'm all right, like everybody else," he finally said. "Just trying not to look so fucking sad. Nobody likes that."

Friday

.

Friday

Thursday night I had gone to the *Philharmonie* to listen to a pianist perform a piece by Philip Glass called *Metamorphosis*. He played it calmly. So calmly that it found time to burrow itself into the mind of the listeners. I wondered how he expected that to work out in a city living on 130 beats per minute.

My neighbors' feet shuffled on the parquet floor during the drawn-out silences. Coughs and sniffles echoed through the megasonic oval hall. I could sense a forced forgetfulness fill the air between the stage and the audience as we were moved gently from one note to the next. The pianist's own page turner was unhappy with the serene composure of the music. She didn't want to turn his notes calmly, casting aside each page with force, as if it was part of the performance. A drop of madness with each paper against the peace of Glass. Until there were no more pages. Until the piece was over.

The following morning, I rotated in my office chair, staring at an open computer program, thinking back on the antagonistic page turner. I figured it was nice of her to try to help the pianist. She did her best to show him that we do not wait that long anymore; our lives filled with relationships that are either much shorter or much faster. She could have played along, but what was the point in pretending.

Around me, the other office chairs were filled with others like me, the same program opened on their screens, yet no one else rotated. I laughed to myself, thinking to cast their screens aside, but waited instead for the clock to strike 5 p.m. I waited and rotated.

After work, I went to see my friend Ruben, one of those relationships that had outlasted a ten-minute techno track. He was telling me about his week at the office while cleaning his apartment, which he kept immaculate. Once he finished with wiping the table between us, he cut up two lines of cocaine on the blacked-out screen of his iPad.

I watched him closely as he cut the clumpy flakes of Colombian sugar. His eyes focused, and his hands working steadily, pushing the powder across the mirrored surface, using an old credit card to sweep everything into a linear pile. He moved in smooth motions, like guiding the bow over a violin and then cutting through the pile in parallel and staccato. There I was, watching a screen again with new music playing in my head. My thoughts built up until I snorted the cocaine.

As the powder hit my nostrils, I sat back in expectation for a few seconds. The initial burn in my nose promptly turned into a numbness on the left side of my face. I saw Ruben's mischievous smile from my seated position as he scuttled closer in his armchair to take his line. I stared at him until he finished his portion, and mine began to truly hit me. When I finally turned away, my vision stalled, my eyelids fluttered, and I had to lean my head back.

The high moved through my body to my mind. As I kept my head back, I shut my shivering eyelids and let the neurons fire inside my brain. *Metamorphosis*, the screens, and Ruben's cuts all fell together into a well-known path. They had nothing to do with me. Why did I care about them? Why did I keep seeing Ruben's smile?

I started to feel good. I was buzzing. The slightest notion of doubt toward anything had left me. The me from a minute ago had split and left the remainder feeling ashamed to have ever been associated with him. I felt the need to go out and show everyone how much better I had become. I also felt like masking that chemical taste in the back of my throat.

"Do you have anything to drink?" I asked Ruben and had already gotten up.

"I should have enough for a couple of gin and tonics. Check for the Bombay in the fridge," Ruben suggested.

I walked to the kitchen. My body felt protected, as if I was a small alien inside of it, maneuvering the human vessel. I was sure of these maneuvers, as sure as I had ever been, no part of me remembering what in the world had worried me earlier. I could barely remember having any worries at all. It may have been in a different life. I poured us two G&Ts.

"You're ready to go after these?" I asked Ruben, handing him a glass.

"Already? I thought we'd chill here for a bit," he said.

I didn't answer but sighed and sat down.

My face had become completely numb. I felt restless but high, rolling my eyes into the back of my head in ecstasy. My favorite thoughts from the day came sprouting out of my mouth, and I didn't feel like stopping them. I started to tell Ruben about the page turner.

"She was just throwing them on the ground!" I exclaimed with all I had, almost crying. "She ripped the pages out in front of him and just threw them away. What a beautiful mess! And he just kept playing."

"Wow! You'll have to let me know next time. I wanna come. I want to make time for this kind of stuff." Ruben smiled and had already prepared a second line of coke.

I took up the metal straw again and felt the second wave throw me even further offshore. Before I knew it, both of us had put on our shoes and stepped out of the house.

We walked out, aiming for Soma, a hipster neighborhood bar, finding our friends Ferat and Yusuf waiting for us at a table in the back. They had two empty whiskey glasses in front of them.

"What did you have?" I asked after greeting them.

"Glenfiddich, twelve years. Do you want one?" said Yusuf.

"I'll just take a beer, I think. You?" I turned to Ruben.

"Yea, a round of beers," said Ruben. Everyone agreed.

Ferat had grown out his black hair and tied it into a man bun since I last saw him. I had nothing to say about it. My high had slowed down a little from the walk, and I wanted to know how their business was doing in Turkey.

"So, how's work?" I asked Ferat. *Don't jitter! Don't jitter!*

"Well," he tucked a strand of hair behind his ear and moved up to the table, "we just met with the crypto guys from the Circle. You know who I'm talking about? They've got some serious money."

"Of course." I had no clue what he was talking about. "Good for you! Great to hear!" I felt my heart flutter and had to contain myself from turning any extremity to the beat playing in the background.

"It's a matter of tactics," Ferat continued. "Local politicians aren't making it easy for us. Education is a touchy subject in Turkey. There's a serious blockade—ah ... yes, just here, thanks!"

Our drinks had arrived, not a moment too early. I grabbed a glass before the waitress could put them down. I took a big gulp, looking her up and down over the edge of my glass. She was wearing a white blouse with revealing cleavage and short shorts. I watched her put the rest of the drinks down without smiling and turn around to walk back behind the bar. All I saw was a tunnel leading from me to her cleavage, an irresistible pull, until a voice interrupted.

"Nice, huh?" I heard Ferat say. I smirked without turning my head.

"How long are you in the city for?" I asked him, still watching the waitress.

"We are leaving tomorrow afternoon."

"Oh, yeah ..." I answered absentmindedly, but then returned sharply. "Wait! You're not coming out with us?"

"Party!" Ruben screamed.

He lifted his pint at me, and we both cheered at the table.

Ferat and Yusuf looked at each other and then back to us. Yusuf pulled up to the table, opened his palms, and shrugged.

"Did you guys take something?" he asked. He had a pitying look in his face, and his tone sounded disparaging.

My partner in conversation until now, Ferat, looked to the ground.

I could not give a shit. "Just a little bit." I flicked the tip of my nose.

"Oh, come on! Seriously, guys?" Yusuf threw his arms up. "I thought we were having a chill night."

"What, you want some?" I asked.

"We're good," Ferat replied.

"Oh, are you going to act all sober now?" I laughed.

"Things are different." Yusuf cut me off, sounding serious. "We're not kids anymore, and this city isn't what's really going on out there. This playground … It's not the real world." He gestured behind himself.

"Okay, party's over." Ruben's voice sounded sarcastic.

"Don't you think it's time to stop and get serious?" asked Yusuf.

"Hey now. It's not like I don't want to talk about it, but the train's left the station. What the fuck do you want us to do at this point?"

I laughed at his question, downing my beer and looking over to see whether Ruben had finished his. Without saying a word to each other, we agreed to get up and pay. We said goodbye to Yusuf and Ferat, the same beat still bouncing from the bar's speakers, and walked out of the Soma.

Our next stop was a house party on the other side of *Prenzlauer Berg*, near *Kastanienallee*. Ruben and I did not talk about what happened at the bar. The high was wearing off, and the words would hit us eventually, but all we mentioned to each other was to take another line as soon as we'd arrive at the party. I did doubt whether Yusuf knew the difference between reality and Berlin any better than us. I tried to put it into words for Ruben but ended up talking about who might be at the party. All for naught, as he abandoned me for his girlfriend the moment we stepped in. I was going to follow and remind him of our agreement but was stopped in my tracks.

A smiley, blonde type of creature appeared in front of me. Her small stature had a frenetic energy around it, and she hugged me before I even realized who it was. When she let go, I recognized Anna, Ruben's girlfriend's Czech friend.

"Hey! What's up?" I asked nervously, allowing for a brief conversation before I had to continue to Ruben.

"So good! So happy to see you. It's been ages! You're coming out with us?" she replied.

"I … I don't really know. Ruben's the one making plans for the night," I said, tapping my nose.

"Ah, cool! What did you have? Ket?" she asked.

"No, just coke," I laughed. "Do you want some?"

Anna blinked her big eyes at me and nodded. She had that kind of sweet face that hid a lot of pain, which I never found myself making much effort in finding out why. I might have found it simply consoling that it made her look a little mad, slightly antagonistic. It was with people like her that I didn't need to check twice, unlike Yusuf.

Anna and I got what we needed from Ruben and hurried into the small apartment bathroom to take a line together while the party banged on outside. She took initiative in cutting the line and did so much less expertly than Ruben. Her hand was sloppy and what should have been concentrated on the phone's screen often looked up at me to go on about a poem she had read in a Turkish-German lit magazine.

This time the high was all right but no longer surpassed the threshold of the previous ones. It mixed with the alcohol that I'd had and convoluted with an ambiguous feeling about the rest of the night. In that triumvirate, the coke had irrevocably lost its dominance. I knew that it meant that all I had was to ride it out. A sober mind would have seen the impeding crash landing, but I ignored it happily. I would keep throwing coal into the fire until the oven burst.

Anna and I returned to our unassuming spot at the party, where I used the opportunity to tell her about the page turner from the Philharmonie. She was impressed by the story, and I loved telling it to her, as she moved her entire body in reaction to my words. When I reached the crux of the story about the falling pages of musical notes, she hopped, pushing her breasts against me and demanding me to go on. I had a difficult time not imagining her naked.

Ruben walked over to us, saying that his girlfriend asked him not to go out with us, his mischievous smile long gone.

Anna turned to me, asking whether I'd still go out, and I replied with certainty that I would. She grinned and asked me to take another line before leaving. I wasn't really sure, but my mouth moved before I could think, and we were in the bathroom once more.

She cut this one even more quickly and carelessly. Chunks of cocaine flew all over the tiled counter of the bathroom. I had lost count of which number line I was on. There was no more high to hit my brain, only a numbness to set me off. I checked the mirror and wiped my nose. We walked out and ran for the taxi.

Next thing I remember was standing on the dance floor of about:blank, staring at Anna's face appearing in between the shockwaves of the dark hall and my mind withering. Around us, shapes of faceless people, outlined by the dust and lasers in front of the altar of our little musical box. The thumping of the techno beat thrusted the plasma inside my body from one corner to the other. We could finally let go, yet danced each by ourselves. The beats, although 130 per minute, reshuffled into a prescribed order, as if running down a checklist and picking up the pages. A drop of sanity against the madness of our mind, at least until the music ended. Until the night was over.

Saturday

Saturday

Rita and I sat in the garden café of the *Einstein Stammhaus* in *Schöneberg*. She had invited me to come and have cake with her, and by doing that, had inadvertently brought me out there for the first time in ages. When the waiter approached, she ordered a pot of Earl Grey for both of us.

"Let's pretend to be an old couple," she said.

It was a sunny afternoon with a sky speckled by those brief clouds that tell of things to come. A few patrons sat scattered around us in the courtyard of the dainty café. Two tables to our left, next to the central fountain, a dapper old man was reading his newspaper under a leafy wooden canopy of white vines. Up and around from him, the middle-aged couple on our right I overheard arguing about an immigration influx somewhere in South America. The topic seemed to make the husband either nervous or excited, as he kept tearing at the crusty part of his croissant on his plate. Diagonally from them, a group of friends in their midthirties sat under a bushy ginkgo. Their table was topped with a fitting number of champagne glasses touching the tangents of a massive carrot cake, missing a handful of fork-size pieces. Their general presences filled and glided all around us, unaffected by themselves. The trickles from the Artemis fountain added to the leaves rustled by the light wind to give the folding of newspapers and low-key conversations a charming background noise. I could have sworn I was in the blooming countryside instead of the heart of West Berlin.

Rita observed the people like I did. She turned in her seat, resting her glance a little longer on the man with the suffering croissant, listening in on their conversation. She shook her head and turned back to me after a while, pouring herself a cup of newly arrived tea without saying anything. She curled her fingers around the cup and carried it to her mouth slowly, blowing the steam off the top. I watched her eyes wander on to somewhere else, to something on our table.

"Get this," Rita nodded at a magazine left behind. "'Changing place, changing time, changing thoughts, changing future.' What is that supposed to mean? What a platitude, amiright? Oooh, I feel so enlightened." She took a sip.

"Where's it from?" I asked, looking down at the magazine.

"Says here some exhibit in Venice. The Guggenheim maybe ...?"

"Hmm." I smiled at her.

Rita smiled back and took another look around. She was wearing a light-blue summer dress that allowed me to make out the shape of her body each time she twisted. As she did, I imagined a drawn line starting at the top of her neck, just below her ear, and stretching across her chest and down below the table, where I could no longer see it.

"So, which one should we get? Carrot cake or lemon cake?" she asked, picking up the menu next to the magazine.

"Carrot, for sure ... right?" I wasn't sure.

"Good choice!" She winked at me, moving a strain of purple hair out of her face and settling my nerves. She put her cup down, leaned over the table, and waved for me to come in close.

"Do you see the old man over there? The one reading the newspaper?" She moved her eyes to the side.

I nodded.

"I wonder what he's thinking. He looks like such a gentleman. I can't imagine him ever misbehaving, but he must have had his wild years, right?"

"Maybe he's pretending," I leaned into the table as well, whispering back to Rita. "I just saw him drop something into his coffee. Maybe that was some GHB, and now he's just pretending to look sober."

Rita laughed, and I wondered whether anyone else could make me feel this funny. Still giggling, she reached for her purse hanging over the side of the woven armchair. She rummaged

56

in there for a few seconds, taking out a small collage notebook, opening it, and pulling out an aluminum strip from one of the creases. She unfolded the strip and put two tiny pieces of paper in front of me.

"*Vamos!*" she said with a seductive smirk.

"Right here? You're fucking crazy!" I lowered my voice and cowered over our table.

"Why not, it's the perfect setting. No one gives a shit. It's so beautiful out, and we'll have time until the tabs kicks in. We'll finish our cake in peace and make it to the museum in time!" She closed her eyes and spread out her arms. She then folded them back together, forming them into a rifle and pretended to shoot me.

"You *are* crazy!" I laughed.

"No pussying out when you're with me! That's the rule!" she said, packing away her pretend rifle.

We took the acid tabs without anyone noticing, just like she said. I was still nervous at first, but seeing that Rita's exclamations hadn't attracted any attention, I trusted that I had no reason to be. Indeed, the garden's patrician audience remained as remarkably unimpressed by Rita's energy as it enthralled me. The newspapers kept folding away at themselves as the large group rang their champagne glasses together. Meanwhile, I didn't even remember what happened to our cake.

We took a taxi to get to the museum. In the car, Rita sat close to me. She put her hand on my leg as the driver took us through a late summer lush *Tiergarten*. I was happy to have gotten rid of the table between us and have her face be closer to mine. I wanted to take in all of its details against the passing scenery before the trip would start. I noticed a slight orange-green discoloration in her otherwise deep hazel irises. I never knew, but her left cheek had certainly more freckles than her right. I could barely pay any attention to what she was saying while counting them. I understood that I had allowed myself to get lost with her without any intention of finding my way back. A dangerous game.

"You're not a flatterer, Ellie. I like that." Rita turned to me while we stood in line to the *Pergamon*. "I haven't heard a single worthless compliment from you. It's kind of refreshing."

"Well ... I dunno," I grinned down at her.

Rita smiled, turning back to the entrance and waving her colorful hair in my face. "Take it or leave it. Up to you," she added.

She leaned her back against me while we waited. I felt a light touch from her dress brush against my leg as I gave her a kiss on the back of the head and wrapped my arms around her.

The people standing around us there were less interesting than the ones we had left behind in the *Stammhaus*. They looked less assorted and intriguing, swarming rather than positioned. About half of them were teenagers from some distant places in the world, their eyes bent down into their devices and not speaking a word. The other half were families with odd numbers of children, wearing unfashionably colorful clothing. It was all but a lingering chatter in the courtyard of the museum. Our sunny afternoon had turned into a warm August's evening.

The acid hit me as we approached the Ishtar Gates inside the *Pergamon*. The first thing that I did was reach out for Rita, who had walked ahead. She stopped still in front of the mosaic entrance to the ancient city of Babylon, and I knew that her trip had started too. She bent her head left and right, looking at the hundreds of animals masoned out of a thousand pieces of tile.

The same dress that had touched me moments ago was now melting into the oceanic blue of the gate. In a moment, I was still unsure of whether it was the drugs or my heart, I saw Rita riding into a field by the sea alongside all of the animals I saw in front of me.

Everyone else had disappeared, as if we had been left alone at the gates of Babylon. I walked up to Rita and grabbed her to stay close to me, not out of selfishness but because I wanted her to know I was there. I touched her and saw her smile. The illumination from the corners of her mouth flooded onto the floor and jumped from wall to wall in the monumental room. I was swimming in the Euphrates with Rita.

"I love this dragon," I heard her say, pointing at one of the animals on the mosaic.

She grabbed my hand and lead me to the next room. Shadows of existences passed around us. If anything distracted my view of her, she was still there, moving through my head. I felt her presence all around. We glided through the gates together, giggling as we did, although she seemed to be moving much more smoothly than me. There was a delicacy to her that I could not emulate even if I tried. Not that I wanted to. I was happy to be the brute in her comparison. She was my muse and I her desperate artist.

We stopped in front of a landscape painting. I told her that I thought it was Tuscany, so we had breakfast there. She asked for another cake, this time—lemon, it seemed more fitting for a warm Italian summer. There was a stream next to the mill, which we followed into the next room.

Rita stood in front of the Pegasus. She stretched out her arms like she did on the chair of the garden and twirled. The whole room twirled with her, her body forming a perfect axis in a rectangular shape. The Pegasus winked at me, and I felt like I should join. But when I got close to Rita, she stopped turning and looked at me. I saw every color in her eyes. I told her, and she laughed.

"You know, he was the one who gave her the hanging garden," said Rita. She took my hand and pointed it at the top of the Ishtar Gate.

59

"Who?" I asked.

"Nebuchadnezzar! He gave his queen the gardens because she missed her home so much," Rita roared at me from a half-crouched position in the middle of the room.

"You would like that, wouldn't you?" I asked.

"Yes," she looked up at me, smiling from ear to ear. "To hell with sexism, I would!"

She touched my hand and skipped into the next room, everyone parting in her way. Rita kept looking at me while walking backward. I would keep doing anything, just to feel her touch once more.

When I turned the corner of the next room, she had suddenly disappeared out of my sight. The walls were still moving, but Rita was not flooding them. I wondered what could have happened to her. Had my reckless following become too much? I needed to stop this nonsense immediately if that was the case! I needed not to lose myself if I were to win her over, although that meant turning cold, something I couldn't fathom. Admit to romance being a false love. There was no way to tell at this point, anyway, so what was the use of never daring. I could risk ending up without her, and what would I be then? Nothing but a fool. I'd rather be the abandoned fool than the one who gave up because of his fright or callous thirst. There would never be a winner, like having tea in a courtyard. I wasn't looking to get better; I looked for a together.

I stopped thinking in front of the tapestry of another Persian king. The tapestry showed him sitting in the middle of his multiple wives and servants, looking resolute. I could not make out whether he was actually happy. What I did see was the pressure of his ancient kingdom. I felt the attention of his pure white robes drawing to him like nothing else on the tapestry.

A song came to my head, not a full song, but a rhythm. It was an electric loop from a song I could not remember the name of. The rhythm spread through my head and soon affected what I saw. The king got up and started to move his hips to the beat. His servants followed suit. The tapestry vibrated with the dancing, and I could not help but snicker.

When I looked away from the tapestry, I found Rita standing right behind me, as if she'd been there all along. She was tapping her foot to the same beat I had just heard. I pointed to her foot without saying a word, walked toward her, and hugged her, nestling my head on her shoulder.

"See? I told you. No one gives a shit," she said. "This city is full of crazy people. We don't even stand out." She paused. "Let's go outside. I want to sit by the river."

She took my hand again and led me back out through the Ishtar gates and out of the museum. We walked across the courtyard and over bridge to the riverbank on the *Hackescher Markt*. There was an accordion player doing his best, but I could barely recognize it as background noise. As soon as we sat down, Rita started to look for something in her purse.

"Do you have any filters?" she mumbled under her breath, turning to me.

I shook my head. She kept digging, taking out our ticket stubs. She was about to roll them up to make filters when I saw her hold still. Something on the tickets had caught her attention.

She read out loud: "I wish I could show you when you are lonely the astonishing light of your own being."

She showed me the quote on the ticket. I looked at Rita, who waited to see my reaction.

"Where's that from?" I asked.

"Hafez," Rita smiled.

The moment that name passed her lip, a fire lit up inside of me. I wanted to dive into the Spree with Rita and to emerge in ancient Babylon. I would build her garden.

Sunday

Sunday

I felt like God for a moment. Lights flashed everywhere. The sound waves coming from the gargantuan musical system cut right through me. Or maybe I was the one coming.

A girl danced in front of me, a young woman, a vision, bending in the flashes. She wore a red baseball cap and a black leather belt that doubled as her only form of undergarment. Each twist of her body moved the light tank top with nothing underneath and played with her nudity. Her movements were calculated and repetitive, perfectly synchronized to the beat. She was the epicenter of our congregation. Whichever face I saw around her, it was focused on her. A gift for the gods, perhaps?

I had taken about 120 milligrams of ecstasy fifteen minutes before I saw the girl with the red cap. I couldn't be exact because I had bitten into Antoshka's 240 milligrams, trying to get about half of it. All I knew was that I had at least another fifteen minutes before being hit by that love.

While waiting, I danced and observed the girl and the others dancing between the towering columns. Most people were dressed down to their shorts or underwear, their sweaty bodies glistening in the thundering dark. The energy was unmistakably sexual, yet I saw no one fucking or even kissing.

We moved all together and yet separately, facing an invisible creator. I was happy in this place, as much as I knew it to be a little fake. I felt like everyone understood each other; at least the objectives were clear.

A tap on my shoulder shot me out of the observation of the red cap. I turned and saw Vi, who gestured at me to join her outside for a cigarette. I followed. The dancers parted in front of us, guiding our path through a wall of turning bodies and out of the dance hall.

The corridors were much darker without the repetitive flashes of the hall. As the music dimmed in the background, the darkness concluded our escape from that surreality. I looked to

Vi, who was leading the way. She must have felt the same thing happening to her but moved on without hesitation. There was, after all, no other way. The decision had been made to step out.

As we did, I was surprised to see that it was still light out. It could have been any time of the day or night, but the evening light surprised me. Vi's rose-blonde hair sparkled in the rays of sun as she held her face to it and lit her cigarette. We walked over to the bar of the garden. It took us a few minutes to say something to each other. In the meantime, I watched others come out of the same corridor for their cigarette. Their sweaty bodies met with the same sun that lit my friend's hair, yet theirs did not sparkle. Most of them squinted and turned away. I saw their pain in dismantling their dancing robes in exchange for fresh air. The robe that made them grand inside had to come off. It made me feel lonely.

"Where are we going after this?" asked Vi. She took a drag of the cigarette and met my eyes. It was the first time we made eye contact since we entered *Berghain*. I stared back into those beautiful green irises that hid so much from me over the years.

"You want to leave already?" I asked.

"Not sure yet. Did you take something?" Vi shrugged.

"Yea, half a pill, twenty minutes ago." I replied. "Wasn't I with you?"

"Hm-hm, no, I was with Vasya, upstairs, next to *Panorama*."

"Aha. How is he?" I asked my friend.

Vi widened her eyes and shrugged once more. A godforsaken green meadow against a simply forsaken orange sky. Why had they never been enough for me? I watched her take another drag of her thin cigarette.

"I got a message from my mom," I said. "Not sure how to deal with it."

Vi continued to look at me but did not ask me about the message. Her eyes wandered off to the side. I turned, following her glance and saw that the girl in the red cap had also walked outside.

"She is very sexy," Vi smirked.

"Do you reckon I should go over there?" I asked before turning back.

"Whatever." Vi scoffed. "If you're nice to her, I am sure she'll talk to you. I'd do it now, before the ecstasy kicks in."

I looked at Vi and smiled. What a loaded suggestion. She did not want me to talk to the girl, or any girl.

"I'll take my chances later." I nudged Vi with my elbow. She sat down on one of the wooden stools by the bar and I took the seat next to her.

She knew what I was doing and grinned. The way she sat, her hair fell over the far end of her neck and revealed her nude shoulder to me. She wore a black bodysuit with dark green laces that spun around her back like a spider's web. Her hair was still wet, and the way she leaned on her arms, she looked like a swimmer getting back on the boat after a dive.

I was triggered by Vi's hair, as long as I did not see her eyes. I wondered if others observed her the way I had been observing the girl with the red cap while dancing. It was most definitely the case. So then, why was I not satisfied? She lit another, pre-rolled cigarette.

"Can I have a drag of that?" I asked.

"Sure, there's a bit of hash in it. Just so you know."

I laughed. "When did you have time to make it?"

She joined in my laughter. "Vasya gave it to me."

I took a long drag.

"Not sure about the crowd today." Vi took back the stub.

"You think so? I thought everyone's very nice." I said.

Vi rolled her eyes. "Of course you do. Check it out, she's looking over at you ..."

I turned to my right and saw that the girl in the red cap was fixated on me. Unlike everyone around her, it seemed that she had been able to keep her robe on. The magic she had inside had not fled her in the sunlight. Only now, I could see her features much more clearly. I saw her say something to her friend, a very fat man in round glasses, her cheekbones forming a mysterious smile and her eyes shooting a glance back at me. I had to guess that she had Mediterranean roots; there was no other explanation for such a pulling scan.

Vi flicked her fuming cigarette, aiming it perfectly to burn my ankle.

"You don't have to drool in front of me." Her voice was sharp.

"Alright, alright. Let's go back inside," I proposed, wiping my ankle.

"No, I am going back inside by myself. You stay out here and do whatever the fuck you want."

With that, Vi's blonde shimmer slid away, inside the club. I barely had any time to consider following her, when the girl in the red cap appeared standing right in front of me. She had a big smile on her face. Her eyes were blue, and her pupils dilated.

"Do you have a light?" she asked.

"Yeah, here," I answered, putting on my most charming smile.

"I am Jill." She said.

"Travy." I said. "Your friends don't mind you talking to me? I see them looking over here."

"Oh, that's just Greg. He's curious to see what I'm gonna do."

"What are you going to do?" I asked.

In an instant, she grabbed my upper arms and drew me closer to her. Her face looked full of mischief. She stood up on her toes, first breathing on my lips and then pressing hers against mine. We kissed with her entire body leaning into me, and I felt her breasts rub against my chest. Her right leg twisted around my right, and she began to grind her hips along my torso. I was surprised that the ecstasy did not kick in at that moment.

As I let go of her lips I went down on her neck. She threw her head back while I held her in my arms like a tango partner. Her tiny tank top drew over to her side and exposed her nipples. As if she had suddenly become aware, Jill pushed me away and took a small step back, readjusting her top. Her look hid an insecurity, but her smile seemed playful. She was still holding my hand, which made me feel wanted.

"What?" I stuttered. "Why … wow."

"Shut up," she countered, shyly turning her head to the side, revealing the side of the neck I was just kissing.

I tried to grab her to come close again.

"What do you think this is, huh?" She smiled, keeping me at a distance. "You don't mind playing this game?" I noticed an accent in her speech. It might have been Italian. "Can I have another cigarette?"

Her other had fallen down. The new one she took between her index and middle finger without looking at me. Another of her friends with purple hair was calling for Jill to join back inside, her head turned.

"Wait, that's it?" I managed to let out before she slipped out of my hand.

"You'll have to find out," she said, and was gone as quickly as she had appeared.

I felt as if everyone had watched what had just happened. I didn't know whether to feel proud or abandoned. She had it all in her hands, but why tease me?

My initial instinct was to follow her; maybe the ecstasy would finally kick in. Maybe I'd get another kiss. Something held me back. I took out my phone.

No new messages

I went through my old messages. I needed to read it again. Not because I wasn't sure of what I had read, but to deal with another portion of what it caused. If only I had gotten it before

I took anything, or the next day.

Your father passed away last night. Call me. - mom

I hadn't been back to the States since last summer. I hadn't spoken to my mother in a month. I was expecting this message any day and still wasn't prepared for it when I got it. Even reading it a fourth or fifth time then, I was unsure of what to do or how to react.

I put the phone back in my pocket and turned to get a drink at the bar. The music was blasting some intense techno track. It might have been by Vril. I could never tell, anyway, and in my state, I was simply content with how relentless it sounded.

I was going to get high whether I liked it or not, taking the decision to let loose for whatever it was worth felt like the right thing to do. I drank from my fresh Gin Mate, a bump of speed, and went back inside. There was no escaping this party.

Finally, it may have been the Mate, the omnipresent beat, the darkness, or even the bump. The ecstasy hit me when I got back to the dance hall. I dove right back into the sea of dancers.

Was I even high?

Was I even conscious?

Moments passed without me having any memory of them. I must have gotten more than the 120 mg. I remembered feeling out of control, out of my mind, dancing with my eyes closed. The music was inside me. I was sure that it was all in my head. There was no tomorrow, only now, there was no me, only a vessel of pure happiness, melting in with everything around it. Until I landed back in my brain, unsure of how much time had passed.

Still high, I felt another tap on my shoulder. This time, it was Jill, her red cap reflecting in the strobe light. I pulled her in to dance with me, but she wouldn't. She stood there and smiled at me. I knew that she saw that I had also melted.

She took my hand and led me downstairs. I followed without question and transcended through her hand holding mine, again. The music kept reverberating from every cell in my body. I felt not only myself flying but her flying with me and my brain balancing on the rope of sanity with little effort. Nothing could hurt me.

Jill led me to a hidden room downstairs. Once inside, she walked over to the wall, arched her back against it and lifted her top. When I approached, she packed me and threw me against the wall, pressing her ass against my crotch. In the next moment I felt her unbuckling my pants as I kept my eyes closed, and then she started to suck me off. Opening my eyes again, I tried to concentrate on the red cap moving back and forth but could barely stand.

I felt pleasure within every inch of my body. When I opened my eyes, she had already taken off her belt and I was taking her from the back. I was barely keeping up. She was pushing against me as I leaned against the wall. We dove onto the couch nearby.

Any time I lifted my head, I saw that same lust she had given me during our first kiss. The memory of her sudden escape aroused me even more. We entangled ourselves violently. I could barely get enough. Each moment screamed for another.

I understood that I could not finish, pulling myself out after what felt like hours, lying down next to her as she laid on her stomach. Both covered in sweat and breathing heavily. She turned her head to look at me. The music came back into effect. I remembered where we were.

My legs were shaking when I got up to find our clothes. I had to sit back down. Jill cuddled up around my waist.

We lay without saying a word. In those minutes, I managed to forget that she was next to me. The exchange in my brain had shifted. I was thinking of tomorrow again and of Vi. For the first time in the last two hours, ambiguous emotions crawled back into my life.

I got up to get water, telling Jill to wait. She sprung up as well and grasped my arm from the side. She felt cold.

"Wait for me outside, all right? In the sun," I said.

We got dressed and parted in the lobby. I rushed upstairs to the dance-floor bar. A fleeting thought crossed my mind that Jill's red cap attracted fewer looks than before. Did I steal her magic?

As I reached the bar upstairs, I felt one last push of euphoria. The comedown was already waving at me from its dead end, but I decided to ride it out dancing. I wasn't as tired as I thought. The sound system embraced me one last time.

A few minutes later, I made it out of the dance hall without hesitation and through the corridors into the garden. No red cap was to be seen. Instead, I saw Vi standing by herself under the small archway next to the bar. She was leaning against the wall with one side, her hip curving beautifully to the other.

I walked up to her, gently touching her side, making her turn around in expectation. I wondered who she might have expected to touch her like this. It was definitely not me.

"Where've you been?" she asked with a look of surprise in her eyes.

"Ah, well, you know," I muttered.

"You said something about a message before. Did you want to talk about it?"

"Meh." I brushed my hand to the side.

"You know I'm with Tom now, right? You can't touch me like this anymore."

"...and where is he?" I asked, still slightly high, biting my lips.

"You know he doesn't like these places."

"But you love him anyway?"

"Look, Travy, shut the fuck up about love, alright. You fucked me up with this in the first place. It's not funny. I know you fucked that red cap. I saw her take you downstairs."

I said nothing but smiled, unable to control it.

"You need to tell me about that message, you asshole. You've been avoiding it."

"My dad died."

Vi's hands fell to her sides and she turned around toward me. "What? Are you serious, Travy?" She gave me a hug. "What the fuck are you doing here? Why are you partying?"

"I got the message when we were here already."

"Fuck man, I'm sorry."

Vi looked down. When she lifted her eyes, I thought of that song I used to play to her when she had a bad day. Some electro tune about enjoying our youth before we get old.

She gave me one more long hug. When she let go, I saw that she wanted to say something but remained quiet. I knew that we both remembered what we used to be for each other in those moments.

"I feel like a joint," I finally said to her.

"Not a bad idea. Do you have anything?" Vi asked.

"Antoshka does. Let's find him."

We agreed and started searching the outside area for our friend. As we did, Vi went farther to the back of the garden and I remained closer to the entrance, where Jill reappeared a minute later, her red cap bouncing through the crowd. She saw me and immediately walked up to me, grabbing my hand to drag me back inside. I turned around in an attempt to tell Vi. The last thing I remembered were her green eyes spying me from afar, falling back into the darkness.

Monday

Monday

I hated this part of town. The buildings looked like a Stalinist wet dream had fucked the color gray. Built sometime between the miserable fifties and the deplorable sixties, East Berlin.

To top it off, this Monday morning's streets were completely desolate, with a thick fog hanging over them. Stalin flirting with Hitchcock.

With a moment's hesitation, I stepped out of the taxi and was hit by a thousand tiny needles of brutal Berlin winter air. I slid my hands into my coat as Drew ran out in front of me towards one of the multiple identical doors staring at us. He held number 54 open for me.

My knees bent further than needed as I ran toward the entrance. Fucking gravity. Granted, I wasn't in my best condition to work against it, as we had been dancing for hours before getting in that taxi. I could sense the hurting happening, without feeling it. It was either the cold or the numbness from the drugs that suppressed the pain.

I threw Drew a quick smile in passing him at the entrance. The laminate flooring creaked under my feet as I stepped into the lobby; bikes and political slogans adorned the walls. It was all too real. I needed a joint.

My mind was foggy. The music from the club was still thumping between my ears. My blood was pulsating, and with it, the world kept rotating on a momentum. I could concentrate on things for a moment before losing my train of thought. I was mostly aware of my own emotions, also pulsating, jogging alongside me. There was happiness, the forgetful bugger, lagging behind front-runner horniness, ahead of the twins cynicism and insecurity.

As we stepped into his apartment, Drew told me to get comfortable on the couch, a different feeling went through my head. I had it the day before, on the eve of going out, hours

81

before arriving at Drew's. I couldn't put my finger on what it was, but knew that I had been escaping it. The music helped, the drugs pushed, and Drew, well, Drew was the bonus. I did not follow his invite for the couch, instead leaning against a wall and watching him turn on an ambient orange-red light in the far corner of the room.

I could make out some wooden furniture to one side and a kitchenette right across from me. Some paintings hung across the short walls, too dark for me to make out, but enough for me to make sure I had never been there before.

"This is the newest BenQ projector," I heard Drew say, turning back to him. "It works in full 4K."

I wasn't sure what he wanted from me but nodded. I was still getting around to comprehending how I had followed him to *Lichtenberg*.

"You said you have some weed?" I asked.

"Mm-hmm, let me get it." He sprinted into a room.

Left alone, I took out my phone but could not concentrate on the screen. Its colors looked smeared and cold. Instead, I held it in front of me and tried to use the front camera as a mirror.

I could provide a little insight as to how I had gotten there. My roommate Chris had introduced me to Drew, a tall and muscular American with that beachboy hairdo, at *Cocktail d'Amore*. He followed me outside when I said that I was going for a smoke, even though he didn't. After making out on the dance floor for a while and then not seeing each other until much later, I didn't hesitate to leave with him. I might not have remembered exactly how I had ended up there, but I remembered why. Drew's shoulders strutted back into the room.

"You wanna roll it?" He showed me two filled plastic bags.

I put my phone away and sat down next to him, watching him fish the weed out of the bag.

"No." I smirked.

"Alright, let me do it." He smiled back.

I replayed how we first locked eyes when we were introduced to each other. Part of that magic was gone, but that didn't matter. It was just so difficult with Americans, always so cool, so nonchalant toward anything they actually liked. And I knew he liked me.

"Can I put on some music?" I put my hand on his thigh.

Drew jolted as if I touched him for the first time and pointed me next to the projector. That was a little too much even for my taste, so I gave him a little slap on the same spot before walking over to the MacBook.

"What's your password?" I doubled down.

Drew finally got up.

"You'd never guess." He winked and took over the computer. If only that wouldn't have worked on me.

I stepped into the middle of the room, waiting for Drew to hit play. His wink still on my mind, I listened to the set that he put on. It started off slowly but quickly picked up and even rekindled my waning rush. The speakers vibrated their power back into me. I started dancing in the middle of the room until a bright light turned on. Dolphins were jumping across the entire wall of popcorn plaster in front of me. Drew had turned on the projector. That joint needed to happen really soon. I closed my eyes and imagined being underwater, swinging back and forth with the music. Audio waves, like ocean waves, the lights flickering through my eyelids like the water's surface.

My head cleared. The thumping subsided. The flashes formed into one ray of light. The music, a release from the dull arrival and my own insecurities. I felt like a child, dancing like no one was watching, although I hoped that Drew was.

When I opened my eyes, nothing had changed. I had just explored the deepest blue with my new dolphin friends, yet Drew was still on the couch.

He sat, his legs spread wide, reaching for his lighter to light the joint, taking a drag and leaned back, looking at me. He exhaled the smoke into the light of the projector, causing a big pumping cloud to expand into the middle of the room. It moved with the music as well. I turned to Drew thinking to convince him to dance with me without saying a word. The idea quickly grew into a desire but I wasn't sure he would understand. He had been so fucking stoic.

He had avoided showing any weaknesses all night, staying in control, the world bending to his masculine will. I knew I had to force him to give it up. I needed his attention. It was time.

With the beat of the music, I inched closer toward Drew, moving my hips from side to side, until I was standing right in front of him. He was definitely watching me. I waited for him to take another drag of the joint. With this drag the music stood still. He inhaled, I leaned down toward him and grabbed the joint out of his hands with my mouth, making sure he felt my grasp on his thighs and shoulders. As I did, I looked deep into his glazed eyes.

I stood back up and took my big drag of the joint without turning to see if Drew had followed me. There were more colorful fish swimming through rugged coral reefs. I closed my eyes again.

The weed weakened the music's intensity in my head. I exhaled. My mind relaxed, but I kept moving.

A touch on my side, above my hip, and then another, from the other side. I felt a breath on my neck. Then a kiss. It sent jitters through my body. The sensation from the weed and the kiss's electricity combined. I shook the grip and turned around.

We were facing each other. He had finally started dancing again, his imagined persona shattered. I had made his animal come out. As we looked at each other, my demons were looking directly at his. I saw Drew's outline against the dim lights of the apartment. Up close, I gave him another kiss before stepping back and taking off my shirt. Drew watched it land on the couch behind him and followed suit until we were both finally topless, again. His time to lead had come to an end. I watched him move to the low notes of the music, moves that were nothing like his voice or expression. Dance could not be faked. I made him beg for the joint out of my hand before I took another deep drag. He growled and blew into the smoke, letting it bounce off of his naked chest. But I simply stepped to him and put my wrists across his shoulders. No more feelings, no more stoics, just the bonus. There would be no tomorrow if we did not sleep.

I want to thank the many friends and family that have supported me and this work along the way. It is dedicated to you all and anyone else who finds it hard to fit in. I hope this book found you at the right time.

If you liked this novella, feel free to rate it on your preferred review website. It does a lot to support independent writers like myself.

To stay up to date on future projects or to send me a message, visit www.anatolischolz.com/contact.

Printed in Great Britain
by Amazon

57623880R00052